ME and MOMMA and BIG JOHN

Mara Rockliff

ILLUSTRATED BY

William Low

To Brooke—
Build something beautiful!

CANDLEWICK PRESS

Momma's first day on the job, she comes home late, trudging up the stairs as if they laid that heavy stone right on her shoulders. She is gray as ashes, from her headscarf to her boots. Even her bouncy beaded earrings have gone dull as dirt.

My big sister hugs her and my little brother says, "You all done building the cathedral, Momma?"

She laughs, but her eyes are tired. "Not yet, angel baby. Not today."

Momma used to work the factory line, right here in the neighborhood. Now an early-early bus takes her across the bridge into the city, all the way down to the yard where they are cutting stone for the cathedral called Big John.

A cathedral is a big, grand, fancy church, and Big John is the grandest of them all.

Momma tells us you could put our whole apartment building in the middle, and it wouldn't even touch the high round ceiling. You could ride an elephant through one of Big John's great bronze doors.

John is my name, too. Momma says she's working
hard to raise us both up right—Big John and little John.
Seems funny, because Big John's *old*. Older than me,
older than Momma. Even older than her momma and
her momma's momma.

"How come it isn't finished yet?" I ask.

"Not meant to be," she says. "Not in my lifetime.
Maybe yours."

On her first day off, Momma's colors come back, bold
and bright. She turns the radio up loud and sings along
with Stevie Wonder while she braids my sister's hair.

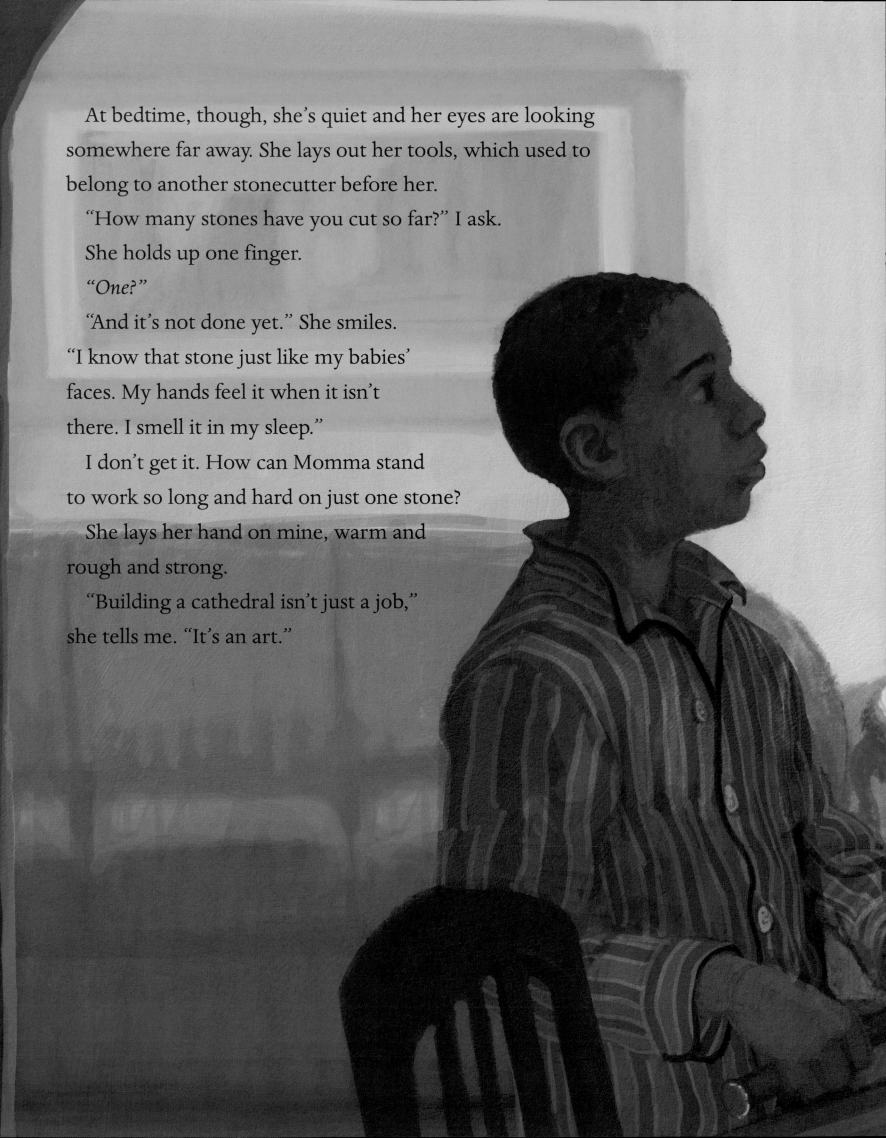

At bedtime, though, she's quiet and her eyes are looking somewhere far away. She lays out her tools, which used to belong to another stonecutter before her.

"How many stones have you cut so far?" I ask.

She holds up one finger.

"*One?*"

"And it's not done yet." She smiles. "I know that stone just like my babies' faces. My hands feel it when it isn't there. I smell it in my sleep."

I don't get it. How can Momma stand to work so long and hard on just one stone?

She lays her hand on mine, warm and rough and strong.

"Building a cathedral isn't just a job," she tells me. "It's an art."

One time, our class went on a trip to the museum. We saw all kinds of art there. Paint art, pencil art. Art made out of clay or colored glass or stone. All the art had names on it, the names of famous artists.

I think of people coming to Big John to look at Momma's stone.

My momma, the artist.

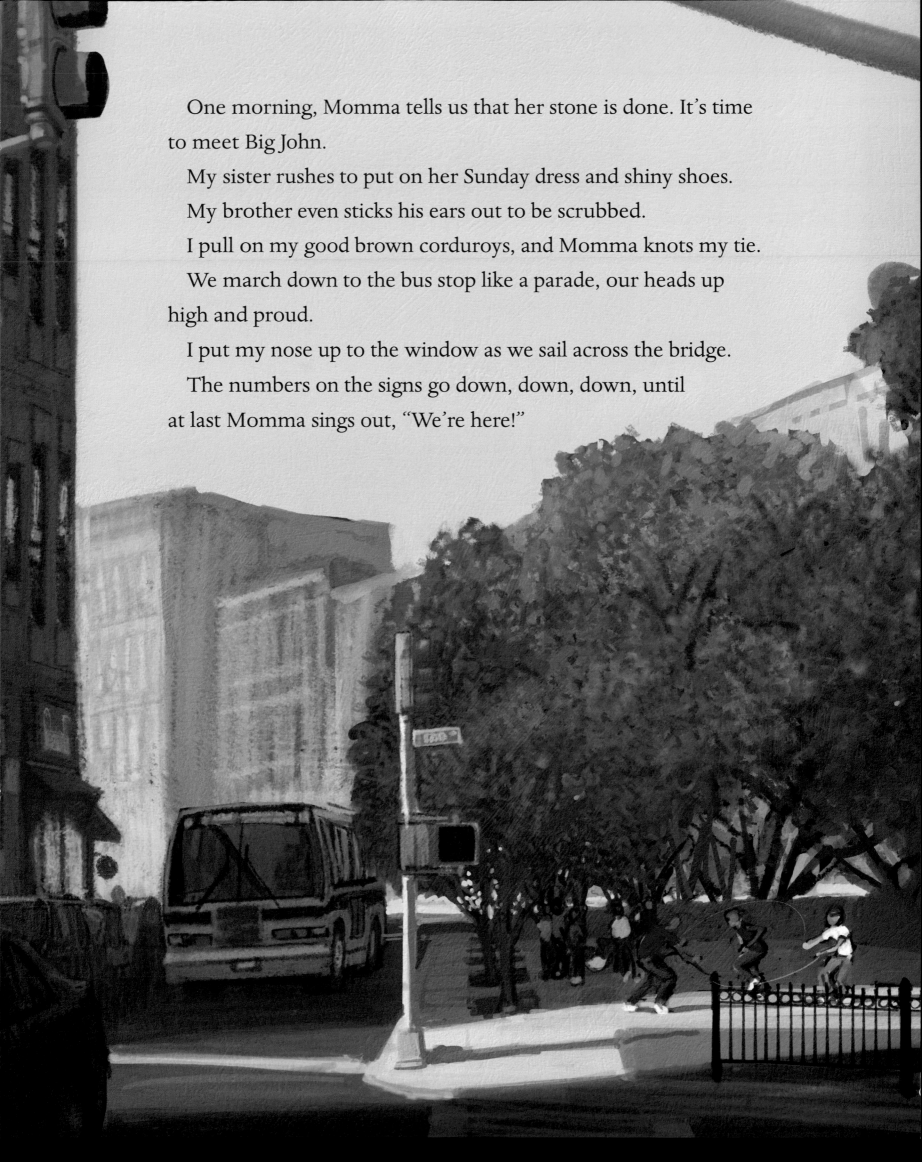

One morning, Momma tells us that her stone is done. It's time
to meet Big John.

My sister rushes to put on her Sunday dress and shiny shoes.

My brother even sticks his ears out to be scrubbed.

I pull on my good brown corduroys, and Momma knots my tie.

We march down to the bus stop like a parade, our heads up
high and proud.

I put my nose up to the window as we sail across the bridge.

The numbers on the signs go down, down, down, until
at last Momma sings out, "We're here!"

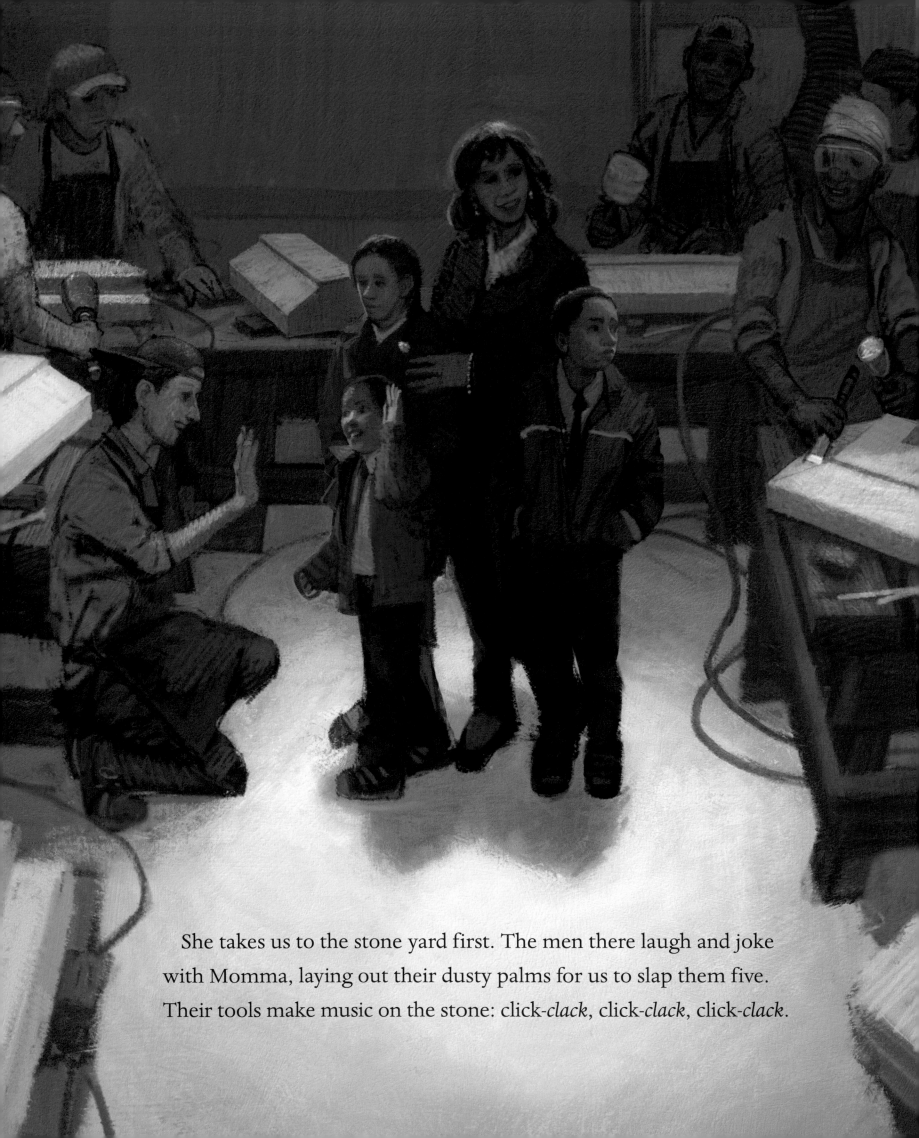

She takes us to the stone yard first. The men there laugh and joke with Momma, laying out their dusty palms for us to slap them five. Their tools make music on the stone: click-*clack*, click-*clack*, click-*clack*.

Then she takes us to her stone.

I walk all around it. From every side, it looks the same: just like all the others.

Something big and gray and heavy settles in my belly. Where is Momma's name? How will all the people know that it's her art?

I drag my feet up the front steps
to the cathedral.

Inside, it feels dark and cool, like
going down into the subway.

High above us, colored windows let in
crisscrosses of light.

"Ooooooooh," my sister says.

My brother bends his head so far back,
he almost falls over.

Even Momma doesn't seem so tall
inside Big John.

When the people start to sing, I think their voices will just fly away and disappear. Instead, each voice lifts up the next, and then the next, each new one held up higher by the ones that came before.

Beside me, Momma's voice joins in the song. I take her hand, and I sing, too.

On the way out, I touch a stone. It's warm and rough and strong, like Momma's hands. I lean in close and breathe the old, old smell.

"See that tower?" Momma points. "My stone is going way up top."
The stones go up and up and up, higher than I can count.

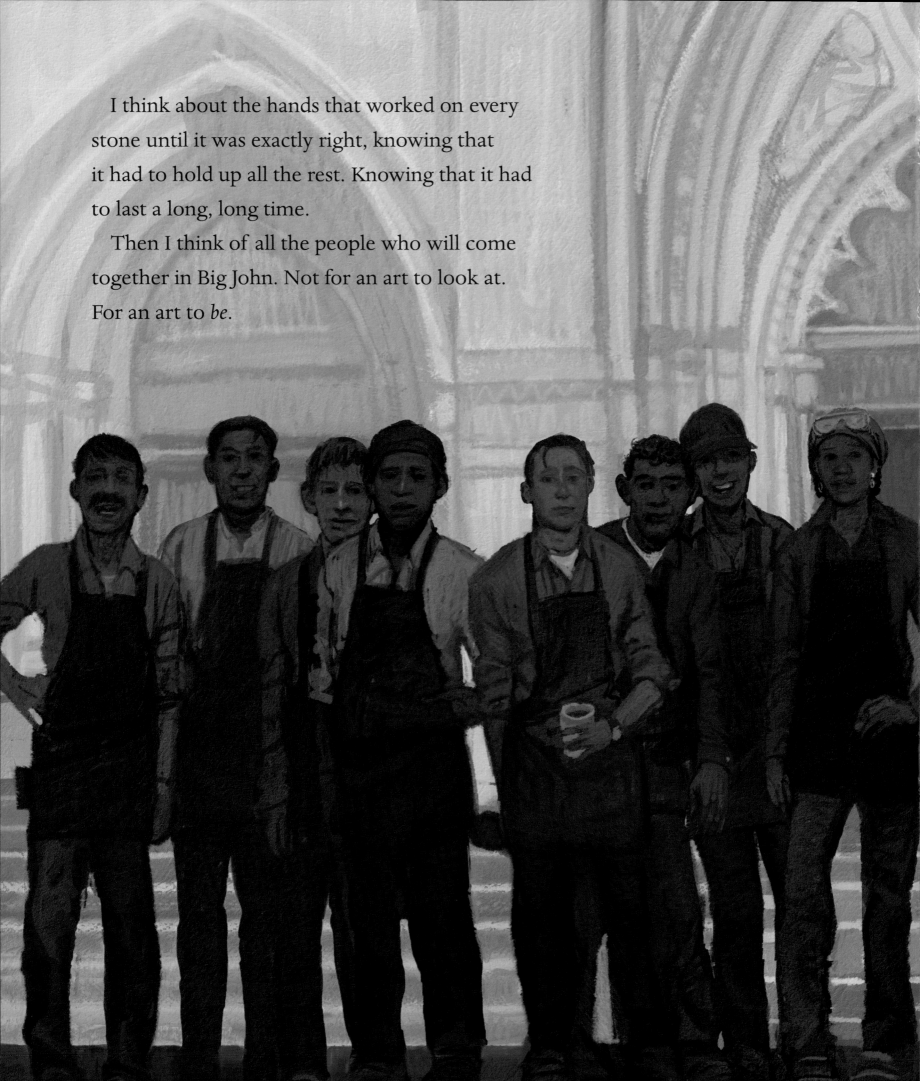

I think about the hands that worked on every
stone until it was exactly right, knowing that
it had to hold up all the rest. Knowing that it had
to last a long, long time.

Then I think of all the people who will come
together in Big John. Not for an art to look at.
For an art to *be*.

And high above the people, Momma's stone touching the sky. Maybe they won't know whose stone it is, but that's okay. We'll know — me and Momma and Big John.

ABOUT BIG JOHN

The Cathedral Church of Saint John the Divine in New York City has two nicknames: "Big John" and "Saint John the Unfinished." It deserves them both.

If you step inside Big John, you'll walk 601 feet before you reach the other end. That's the length of two football fields—with room left for the football, too. This gigantic space has held everything from parades of llamas, elephants, and pythons to a tenement apartment that once housed a family of nine.

Workers laid the cornerstone for the cathedral in 1892. As Big John began to rise, the horse-drawn wagons rolling past were jolted by thrill-seeking New Yorkers trying out the latest crazes—bicycles and automobiles. World War I slowed the building, but as soon as it was over, Broadway stars and famous athletes jumped in to raise needed funds, led by an energetic young lawyer named Franklin Delano Roosevelt. Then came World War II. This time, when construction stopped, it wouldn't start again for forty years.

Why the delay? New York was in trouble. In the neighborhood around Big John, many people were hungry, homeless, out of work. It seemed wrong to spend money on stained glass and tall, fancy towers when it could go to help people in need.

Then, in the 1970s, the dean of the cathedral had a new idea. Young New Yorkers needed jobs. Why not hire them to build Big John? In Europe, stonework was a dying craft. He would bring masters over to teach stonecutting and carving. Their craft would be revived, young people would have paying jobs and learn a skill, and construction would begin again at last.

In 1982, with great fanfare, the first new stone was laid. The famous tightrope artist, Philippe Petit, walked across a wire twenty stories high, holding a silver trowel.

The apprentice program lasted twenty-five years. Then the money ran out again, and construction stopped. But life goes on inside Big John, whose mission is to serve as a house of prayer for all people and a center of thinking, creativity, community, and justice. Under its temporary roof, over the years, thousands of people have gathered to be fed and sheltered, to celebrate and mourn, to open their minds to new ideas and their hearts to joy.

One of the apprentices was a young mother, Carol Hazel, who inspired *Me and Momma and Big John*. "Stonecutting is in my blood," she says today. "The cathedral is a beautiful thing, and beautiful people helped build it."

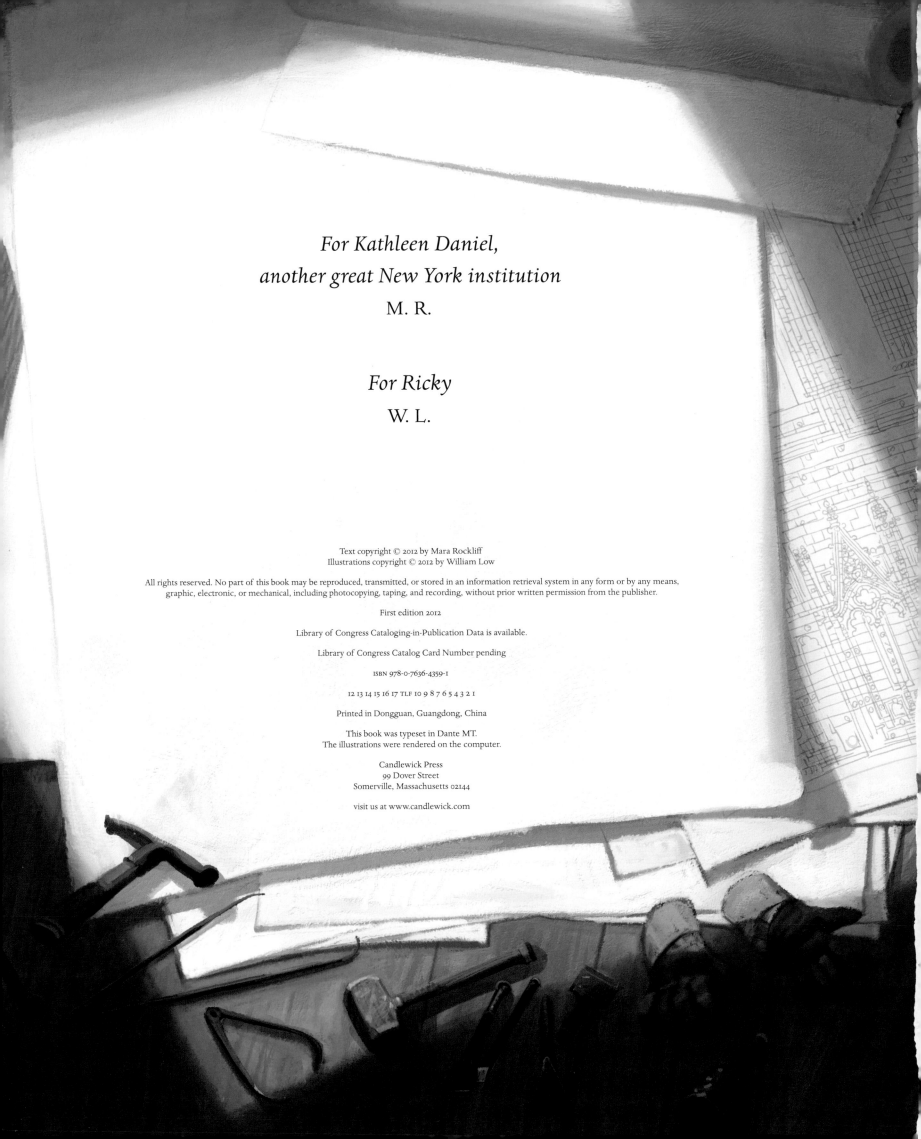

For Kathleen Daniel,
another great New York institution

M. R.

For Ricky

W. L.

Text copyright © 2012 by Mara Rockliff
Illustrations copyright © 2012 by William Low

First edition 2012

Library of Congress Cataloging-in-Publication Data is available.

Library of Congress Catalog Card Number pending

ISBN 978-0-7636-4359-1

12 13 14 15 16 17 TLF 10 9 8 7 6 5 4 3 2 1

Printed in Dongguan, Guangdong, China

This book was typeset in Dante MT.
The illustrations were rendered on the computer.

Candlewick Press
99 Dover Street
Somerville, Massachusetts 02144

visit us at www.candlewick.com